Erma Bombeck: At Wit's End

Allison Engel and Margaret Engel

A Samuel French Acting Edition

SAMUEL FRENCH

FOUNDED 1830

SAMUELFRENCH.COM
SAMUELFRENCH-LONDON.CO.UK

FOR PRODUCTION ENQUIRIES

UNITED STATES AND CANADA
Info@SamuelFrench.com
1-866-598-8449

UNITED KINGDOM AND EUROPE
Plays@SamuelFrench-London.co.uk
020-7255-4302

Each title is subject to availability from Samuel French, depending upon country of performance. Please be aware that *ERMA BOMBECK: AT WIT'S END* may not be licensed by Samuel French in your territory. Professional and amateur producers should contact the nearest Samuel French office or licensing partner to verify availability.

MUSIC USE NOTE

Licensees are solely responsible for obtaining formal written permission from copyright owners to use copyrighted music in the performance of this play and are strongly cautioned to do so. If no such permission is obtained by the licensee, then the licensee must use only original music that the licensee owns and controls. Licensees are solely responsible and liable for all music clearances and shall indemnify the copyright owners of the play(s) and their licensing agent, Samuel French, against any costs, expenses, losses and liabilities arising from the use of music by licensees. Please contact the appropriate music licensing authority in your territory for the rights to any incidental music.

IMPORTANT BILLING AND CREDIT REQUIREMENTS

If you have obtained performance rights to this title, please refer to your licensing agreement for important billing and credit requirements.

ERMA BOMBECK: AT WIT'S END was first produced by Arena Stage in Washington, D.C., on October 9, 2015. The performance was directed by David Esbjornson, with sets by Daniel Conway, costumes by Elizabeth Hope Clancy, lights by Rob Denton, sound by Rob Milburn and Michael Bodeen, and dramaturgy by Jocelyn Clarke. The Stage Manager was Marne Anderson and the Assistant Stage Manager was Rachael Albert. The Associate Director was Anita Maynard-Losh. The cast was as follows:

ERMA BOMBECK . . . . Barbara Chisholm

CHARACTERS

ERMA BOMBECK – a dynamo with an easy laugh.

SETTING

We see her in the Bombeck home in suburban Dayton, Ohio.

TIME

The present, and various times from 1962 – 1996.

PRE-SHOW ANNOUNCER. *(Voiceover.)* Ladies and gentlemen, thank you for silencing all your electronic devices. [NAME OF THEATER] is pleased to bring back humorist Erma Bombeck. Let's give her a warm [NAME OF CITY] welcome.

> *(As the audience applauds,* **ERMA BOMBECK** *enters from the side of the stage in a pool of ethereal light. She wears a shirtwaist dress.)*
>
> *(Sound: Music accompanies the light.)*
>
> *(***ERMA** *acknowledges the audience with delight.)*
>
> *(***ERMA** *steps out of the light and enters the playing space, which has a door on either side of the set. The main part of the playing space is a living room with shag carpeting, a bedroom with a double bed and a kitchen with a table and chairs. The bed's headboard holds* **ERMA***'s books. There is an ironing board, an iron with a ridiculously long cord, and a laundry basket filled with clean clothes. There's a vacuum cleaner, a telephone in the bedroom, and an easy chair and side table in the living room.)*
>
> *(Music fades.)*

ERMA. Oh gosh. It's really wonderful to be here.

Looking back, it's hard to figure out how I got to suburbia. One moment you're studying for a college degree. Then, boom! You have a baby in your arms.

Once you dreamed of being a foreign correspondent. Then, boom! Chef Boyardee is as exotic as it gets. I was blazing a trail all right, but it only led from the laundry room to the sink.

(Sound: Children fighting, yelling, laughing. All talk over each other in a cacophony with a rare single line heard.)

(ERMA *signals to the audience to wait. She can't talk right now. She makes her way to the kitchen.)*

(To unseen children.) Sit up straight and eat your breakfast.

If your brother stole your fork, use your spoon.

Elbows off the table.

Please don't feed the dog.

Keep you feet to yourself.

Don't feed the dog.

Careful, you're going to spill.

I *told* you not to feed the dog.

What are you wearing now?

Go upstairs and change.

Don't worry about that tooth, it's gonna come out sooner or later.

It's time to go. Get your books.

Bill, hurry up! The kids are going to be late.

(To an unseen Bill.)

Bill, there's a first time for everything and it's yours for driving the carpool.

I know, transporting children is your 13th favorite thing, right between eating lunch in a tearoom and dropping a bowling ball on your foot. Just remember, this means you have to bring the car to a complete stop and open the door for them. They are small children, not sacks of mail.

(ERMA *opens the front door for Bill.)*

(Addressing unseen children.) Your shoes are on the wrong feet. I thought I told you to change. Don't forget to give your note to the school nurse. Remember, 7 times 8 is 56. Do you have your lunches, your coats, your glasses, gym clothes, pens, pencils, milk money and bookbags? Love you all, goodbye.

(**ERMA** *shuts the door. She attempts to speak, but is interrupted by…*)

(*Sound: Doorbell.*)

(**ERMA** *answers the front door.*)

Yes? What. You can't hate school yet. It's your first day.

(**ERMA** *shuts the door.*)

Welcome to my mornings. Breakfast made me wonder why I take pride in cooking, if they don't take pride in eating?

Children are the most suspicious diners in the world. How can a child eat yellow snow, kiss the dog on the lips, chew gum that he found in the ashtray…and refuse to drink from a glass his brother just used?

Although one child did learn something this morning. If he wants an extra pancake, just cough on his sister's plate.

How did I end up in suburbia? It seems like ancient history now.

(*Newsreel music: World War II march music in the style of "The Caisson Song."*)

Rosie the Riveter gives up her factory job to a returning G.I. and soon answers to a new name: "Mom." This Mom was part of the biggest, boomiest boom in history.

And just where does our little Rosie settle down?

(**ERMA** *puts on pop-bead pearls and a frilly apron from the laundry basket.*)

In our nation's newest community, Cherrywood Acres in good old Dayton, Ohio. Split level ranches come complete with timesaving appliances. And there's plenty of room for that station wagon in the garage. Boy, America's moms truly have it all – a carefree life far from the stress and crowds of the big city.

(*Sound: Harp glissando – as often used in cheesy '50s television jingles.*)

(ERMA dances along as she sings this advertising jingle.)

ERMA.

WHAT A DREAM OF A KITCHEN FOR YOU
WHAT A DREAM OF EASY LIVING THAT'S NEW.
AND WHAT MAKES IT GREATER,
IT'S ALL WARDINATOR, SO MODERN, SO USEFUL, SO YOU.

(Sound: Harp glissando.)

(ERMA holds her last dance pose as the harp glissando plays.)

ERMA. *(Ironically.)* This was me in my house, all the time.

(ERMA takes a magazine, Better Housekeeping, circa 1964, from the table by the easy chair. The cover features a model housewife wearing an apron and a frozen smile. ERMA shows the audience the cover and mimics the smile. She vacuums, teetering on her heels and looking to the model housewife for approval. She trips over something on the floor.)

(Sound: Crunching of Army men being vacuumed up.)

(ERMA turns off the vacuum.)

(In model housewife's voice.)

(Patronizing.) It often works best if you pick up the Army men first.

(ERMA gets down on her knees and picks up Army men.)

Whatever doesn't kill you now, comes back a few days later and tries again.

(ERMA continue vacuuming and then suddenly stops in horror.)

(To the model housewife.) Oops! I almost sucked up one of the hamsters. He must be trying to escape the boys' room to cleaner air. *(Pause.)* There he goes!

(To audience.) I bet she never passes varicose veins off as textured stockings. Or thaws pork chops by putting one under each armpit? She spends her time lecturing us with fashion do's and don'ts, rules for entertaining and beauty hints written like they are a matter of life and death.

Add them all up and you've got dozens of ways to be considered a failure.

In my house, I didn't worry about perfection. For Halloween, I'd put the cat on my son's head and send him out as Davy Crockett. Or dot my daughter's face with lipstick and call her a contagious child.

There are very few women like that, but you wouldn't know it from reading magazines, watching television or going to the movies.

There was one in our neighborhood. When her kids played at our house, they wrote thank you notes for a drink out of the garden hose.

But on the other hand, "Mrs. Perfection" and her kids didn't communicate. I speak fluent child:

If you don't stop crossing your eyes, they are going to freeze that way.

Put your sweater on. Don't you think I know when you're cold?

When that lawn mower cuts off your toes, don't come running to me.

> (**ERMA** *points to the cover with the model housewife.*)

Those magazines never answer the real questions, such as: Is it better to put your groceries away after each visit to the store or do what we do, and eat them directly from the car?

And those endless stories on dieting! I have been on a diet for twenty years. I've lost a total of 789 pounds. I should be hanging from a charm bracelet.

(**ERMA** *takes off her apron and pearls.*)

I did try exercising for a while. The other women in the class were so thin that buzzards followed them to their cars. Every day I'd groan, stretch, sweat and strain until I thought I was going to die. But once I got those tights on, it got better.

(**ERMA** *takes off her high heels.*)

The only plus about exercise was that I got to hear heavy breathing again.

I was a willing prisoner. Signed up young. I didn't want to be the older mom, the one fighting her kid for the baby food – or spanking my toddler for coloring on my Social Security check.

(**ERMA** *sets up the ironing board and iron.*)

I was kinda hoping that over the years, we'd be able to figure out the mom thing. You know, the seesaw between work and home. But on that front, nothing seems to have changed.

You don't mind if I do two things at once, do you? Force of habit.

How did I find time to write?

(**ERMA** *thinks of something and gets a notebook from the headboard.*)

(*She takes a pen out of her purse. It doesn't work and she uses a lipstick from her purse.*)

(*As she writes.*) "Motherhood is the world's second oldest profession, but unlike the first, there's no money in it."

(*To audience.*)

There are some similarities. Almost everything you do is behind closed doors and no one knows what you do or how you do it. I loved being a mom, but to the outside world, I was simply a housewife. Housewife, what a concept, a woman married to a house.

But I liked being here when the kids got home, and *trying* to cook a mediocre dinner that was ready when Bill walked through the door. You know, a stable, well-organized life. For them, at least. I didn't need to sleep. I did, however, need to iron. At least the parts that were going to show.

(**ERMA** *irons Bill's shirt.*)

My husband and I had both worked in a newsroom, but after we got married, he'd read me the daily paper: the current weather in Nome, Alaska, what Dear Abby said to the woman whose husband dressed in the closet, the high school basketball scores, why South bid seven hearts, and what Lucy did to Charlie Brown. It was obvious. I couldn't read a newspaper by myself.

Every day, my family returned from the outside world, threw open the door, looked me straight in the eye and asked, "Is anyone home?"

If life is a bowl of cherries, what was I doing in the pits?

Yes, I signed up for this life sentence. But at least a lifer gets a parole hearing every few years and the hope of a pardon.

The whole thing was – and is – ridiculous. If you can't make it better, you had better laugh at it.

And if you can laugh at it, you can live with it.

Housewives have important things to say, but there's usually no one to talk to but the tropical fish.

(*Sound: Doorbell.*)

(*Beat.*) And a certain variety of shark.

(**ERMA** *opens the front door to an unseen man.*)

Hello.

(*To the audience.*)

Biff Blanchard. Casualty Mutual.

(*To Biff.*)

No, I don't think we went to school together. Not unless you wore a plaid jumper and knee socks.

(Pause.) It was an all-girls school.

Sure, go ahead and call me Edna. Many people do.

The "warm circle of insurance protection?"

I'm sure your polls are right, Biff, but I haven't trusted polls since I read that 62 percent of women had affairs during their lunch hour.

(**ERMA** *shuts the door.*)

I've never met a woman who would give up lunch for sex.

(Thoughtfully, thinking about Biff Blanchard's words.) Where would you be if something happened to the mister?

My dad died when I was nine years old. Here's what happens. You take all your clothes out of your drawers. Men take all the dressers and tables away. Even your beds go back to the store where your dad bought them. Then, they drive his car away.

(**ERMA** *returns to the ironing board.*)

My mom was only twenty-five years old. She had me when she was sixteen. So we moved back in with her parents. I got dumped on aunts and uncles a lot. It was nothing for me to be at the local tavern with them til midnight.

We adapted. We coped.

It was the Great Depression. Mom put on overalls and worked in a factory, wrapping copper around engines. We shared her old bedroom. There wasn't room for my half-sister – my best friend – and she had to go live with far away relatives. I didn't see her again for seven years. We used to tap dance together.

When I was in kindergarten, I had a job tap dancing on the radio. The Kiddie Review show. Tap dancing in the 1930s was so popular – thank you, Shirley Temple – that people all across America turned on their radios just to hear that sound. I got paid $2 a week and that $2 mattered.

And I kept tap dancing all my life.

It was up to me to find new friends. They were much older, and they made me laugh. Mark Twain. Dorothy Parker. Robert Benchley.

They taught me that if you're living with sadness, at least you can escape by writing. I started writing early, and by the time I was fifteen, I had my first job at the *Journal Herald* in Dayton. Obituaries. It may not sound like much, but as my mother told our neighbor, "You try to get all those people to die in alphabetical order."

Eventually, I got my own beat: Compiling household hints for a column called *Operation… Dustrag*. Which was strange, because my idea of housework is to sweep the room with a glance.

"To revive chintz, simply add a small amount of paraffin to a clear starch. Then, iron your chintz on the right side so it will have a glaze."

One horrified woman wrote me that if her curtains had wicks they would have burned right through Advent. To this day, homemakers are still trying to salvage bits and pieces of the damage I caused.

Truth is, it's hard to find humor in household hints. Not that I didn't try. I once wrote: "If you want to get rid of stinking odors in your kitchen, just stop cooking." But writing about household hints was a dead end.

Much more daring was honestly describing a typical day for a housewife. No one had the courage to write that.

You see, women in the 1960s were not admitting certain things to themselves. Your life was to serve your husband and your kids and you better not forget it. Point out the flaws, you got branded as a substandard wife and mother. Like most of us, I was willing to conform.

I had been hiding my hopes and dreams in the back of my mind. It was the only safe place in the house.

From time to time, I got them out and played with them. Reveal them to others? No, they were too fragile.

When my youngest started kindergarten, I was thirty-seven years old and my excuse for everything had just gotten on the school bus.

I began to dream about a column that used humor to tell the truth about my life.

Writing a column was what I could do. I was too old for a paper route, too young for Social Security and too tired for an affair.

Besides, Bill and I couldn't support three children with two overbites on one high school teacher's salary. Several of my friends also decided to get paying jobs. A few did it for the money. Most because they needed the rest.

I took my idea to our local weekly. Guess what? The editor bought it. Three dollars a column, don't spend it all in one place. My beat started at the crabgrass in the front yard and ended at the back porch.

(**ERMA** *puts the iron away.*)

I had no particular words of wisdom, just common sense advice like: "Never trust a doctor whose office plants have died."

Mostly, my column asked questions. Why is motherhood called the most important job in the world, if no one wants to know how it's done? I also wondered why there was a rectal thermometer in the cookie jar, but I tried to stay focused on bigger things.

I got myself an office, also known as our bedroom.

(**ERMA** *locates a portable typewriter under the bed.*)

(She puts the typewriter on the ironing board.)

A room of one's own.

It's a miracle I became a writer at all. By the time I was in my teens, I had a new step-dad, and he and Mom decided college wasn't for me. Neither of them had graduated from high school so they didn't see the use. Their plan was for me to work as a secretary until I could find a husband. Mom never thought writing could be a career.

*(**ERMA** throws the carriage return.)*

(Sound: Ding!)

Such a beautiful sound.

(Sound: Children bounding up stairs, yelling and laughing. All talk at once. Children's voices sound like a cacophony with a rare single line heard.)

They're back.

*(**ERMA** types quickly.)*

(Reads.) "If the Virgin Mary had lived on our block, we would have said 'Of course *she* has time to go to the dentist. *She* only has one kid.'"

*(**ERMA** listens with her head cocked.)*

(To the door.) One at a time, please!

The hamster accidentally FELL in the toilet?

You used the glass thingy from the punch bowl?

And it broke?

(To the audience.)

Perfect. Insanity is hereditary. You can catch it from your kids.

(Sound: Flush.)

CHILDREN. *(Voiceover.)* Mom!

ERMA. Emergencies do arise, no doubt about it, but some guidelines must be established.

(To the door.) Before you bother me while I'm working, ask yourself: Will Mom carry out her threat to move to another city and change her name?

Now, here are the rules for the rest of the afternoon: If there is blood to report, consider these questions. Is it yours? Your brother's? Is there a lot or a little? Is it on the sofa that is not Scotch-guarded?

Now go watch TV!

(To audience.)

God bless television. You put your kids in front of it and it's like hypnotizing chickens. All of our kids could sing beer commercials before their eyes could focus.

Since our children mothered every animal they could trap in a Mason jar, we attended a pet funeral nearly every week of our lives. There was a small lizard who lived in a terrarium on the back of the toilet, whom I suspected died of 'flush anxiety.' We put to rest a pet beetle. Had there been an autopsy, it would have revealed half of our shag carpet.

The most poignant services were the ones conducted for deceased guppies at the toilet bowl. We'd all stand around the rim staring into the water and I'd ask if the little guy had a name. They always did.

Then I would ask each child to say something appropriate and nice about the fish. Sentiments came to mind like, 'I'm sorry I fed you pizza, Ethel.' 'Ethel never bit anyone.' 'Ethel didn't smell until last night.'

Parents bear some blame. We allow animals to join our families. We do this to teach children about love, responsibility and even grief. My friend lost a beloved pet and felt duty-bound to explain the life and death cycle to her 5-year-old daughter. "Honey, we can all be happy now that Frisky is up in heaven with God." Her daughter replied with no emotion, "Mom! What's God going to do with a dead dog?"

(**ERMA** *goes back to the typewriter.*)

Ohio University didn't think I had much writing talent and Mom and step-dad hoped I'd give it up, but I decided to try again.

This time, at the Catholic school, the University of Dayton, I heard those three little words I longed to hear. "You. Can. Write." Now, I'm not saying that was the only reason I converted to Catholicism and started eating fish on Fridays, but those three words were my green light.

During a school break, the *Dayton Herald* hired me. I was in heaven – surrounded by real writers. Then, copy girl met copy boy. Bill Bombeck also worked at the paper.

The next thing I knew I was wearing an oversized wedding dress that I bought on sale. And my mom was smelling like the baked ham she cooked to take to the reception.

That was our last good meal for a while. Turned out I was a terrible cook. Almost immediately, Bill told me he wanted to exchange some of our wedding gifts for something useful: a vending machine. The one thing he didn't want to return was our smoke alarm. It told him when our dinner was ready.

When our kids misbehave, I tell them if they don't shape up, I am going to put them to bed *with* supper.

(*Sound: Knocking at the door.*)

(*A note slides under the door.*)

(*Reads the note.*) "Can we have $1.50 to go to McDonald's?"

(*To audience.*)

Most children's first words are Ma-Ma or Da-Da. Ours were, "Do I have to use my own money?" And, like all children, they drove us crazy to buy things they saw on TV. In fact, our kids wouldn't eat anything they hadn't seen dance on a screen.

> *(Sound: Children pounding on the door.)*

I know! You're waiting. McDonald's isn't going anywhere.

> **(ERMA** *smiles guiltily. She finds a dollar in her pocket, and searches through the pockets of clothes in the laundry basket for spare change. She counts coins in her hand. She's short. She pulls a pair of penny loafers from under the bed and removes the dimes. She slides the money under the door.)*

(Sarcastically.) Thank you, Mom!

Sometimes I wonder if children are like waffles. Should the first one be used to season the grill and then tossed out? The misshapen, the one with hard edges, the one that falls apart…they are all miracles.

I think every mother has a favorite child. She cannot help it. I have one – although right now, I'm not sure any of mine are on the list.

My favorite child is the one who was too sick to eat the ice cream at his birthday party, had measles at Christmas and wore leg braces to bed because his feet toed in.

My favorite child is the one who screwed up the piano recital, misspelled 'committee' in a spelling bee, ran the wrong way with the football and had his bike stolen because he was careless.

My favorite child said dumb things for which there were no excuses.

She was selfish, immature, bad-tempered and self-centered. She was vulnerable, lonely, unsure of what she was doing in this world.

The favorite child is always the same one, the one who needs you at the moment for whatever reason – to cling to, to shout at, to hug – but mostly, to be there.

When I started writing, I thought it was just my life that was zany. After the first columns ran, everyone on the block confessed it was their lives, too.

Then my old paper stole me away with fifty bucks a pop. I called the new column *At Wit's End*.

> *(Sound: Ringing phone.)*

> *(ERMA answers the phone.)*

Hello? Yes, uh huh. Yes, I could do three columns a week. What? Really? Thirty-six papers? Are you serious? *(Long pause.)* Sorry, I'm just a little speechless for once. O.K., yes. Thank you. Thank you.

> *(ERMA hangs up. She dials the phone.)*

Bill, I just got a call from Newsday. The people there want to sell my columns to papers around the country! They think it could run in – are you sitting down? – thirty-six papers. Thirty-six. You can quit painting houses in the summer. And I'll be *At Wit's End* three times a week.

> *(ERMA hangs up.)*

I thought that weaving a career into the fabric of a traditional family would throw five lives into upheaval. It didn't cause so much as a ripple. I started writing at 8:30 a.m. and I closed up shop in time to make dinner.

No one noticed the dynamo racing through the house faster than aspirin through the bloodstream, able to leap over three kids to get dinner to the table. They didn't have a clue that the mild-mannered woman who sewed in name tags at midnight, by day wrote columns and books, never missing a deadline. When one of our children was asked at school what I did, he said I was a syndicated Communist.

I think so much comes down to the kind of marriage you have. No matter how many fans I had across the country, there was always Bill to keep me grounded. He kept teaching, didn't manage my career and stayed his frugal self. Heaven forbid we should throw something out. Or waste electricity.

Our guests saw him turn off the porch light before they reached their cars in the driveway. By his description, our house was lit up like a pleasure boat cruising the Potomac. My friends actually didn't know his first name. They only heard me refer to him as The Prince of Darkness.

(**ERMA** *puts on Bill's shirt.*)

His tours through the house every evening became legendary. "Who's in the kitchen?" Click. "Who's in the hall closet?" Click. "Who's in the bedroom?" Click.

Then we would wait for his dramatic tally. "I have just turned off thirteen lights."

That speech was not his only long-running performance. Bill had dinner-table lectures that became as familiar to us as the Pledge of Allegiance.

Why Don't You Want Your Father to Have a Lawn?

Two minutes, fifty-five seconds. This was a real heart-tugger in which Dad recaps his failure to triumph over bikes, sleds, plastic pools, football games, cars, wagons, dogs and all the little perverts who cut across his lawn just to make him paranoid.

I'm Paying You Kids an Allowance to Breathe. Three minutes, eighteen seconds. This was a group participation lecture.

"Do you know how much money I made when I was a child?"

"Five cents a month."

"Five cents a month," he said as if he hadn't heard them.

"And do you know how old I was when I got my first car?"

"Twenty-three years old."

"Twenty-three years old and I bought it myself. And do you have any idea how much I had to buy with five cents a month?"

"You had to buy all your own clothes, books, tuition, rent and pay for your entertainment."

"And do you know what I did for entertainment?"

"You changed your underwear?"

"Hey, don't ad lib."

Thank goodness Bill was always a good sport about me making jokes. I once told my readers, "God created man. I could have done better."

> (**ERMA** *takes off Bill's shirt.*)

I got lucky, because really, women shop for a bathing suit with more care than they do for a husband. The rules are the same. Look for something you'll feel comfortable with. Allow for room to grow.

For all those years, my wedding ring did its job. It led me not into temptation. It was a status symbol in the maternity ward. It was a source of relief to a dinner companion. And it reminded my husband many times at parties that it was time to go home.

I could never explain how our marriage worked. Neither could most of our friends. We took vacations together and we took them separately. It all came down to trust. I couldn't light the water heater and he needed me to send out the Christmas cards, so we were pretty secure.

When I last checked, we were members in good standing of your average screwed-up family. And I was happy to own up to it.

I wasn't one of those women who pretend that being a wife and mother is simple if you only try hard enough. It wasn't easy. Any parent who has been on a trip with a child who kicks the seat for fifty miles and throws his shoes out the window has definitely considered abandoning him at the next Shell station.

Not all readers liked my honesty. I started getting a few angry letters. "Why did you have children?" ... "You're a terrible mother!" ... "I feel sorry for your family!"

I assure you there was love in every line I wrote.

There is something I want to share with you. It's a letter I received from a mother in prison.

> (**ERMA** *looks in the headboard and finds an oft-folded letter.*)

(Reads.) "Dear Erma Bombeck: You may not want to hear from the likes of me. I am serving a life sentence for killing my own child. I have read all of your columns in our library, several times. Had I known mothers could laugh at these things, I probably wouldn't be where I am today."

> (**ERMA** *returns the letter.*)

I keep this letter to remind me that there is a thin line that separates laughter and pain.

I kept plugging away at the column, trying not to whitewash motherhood. God knows women didn't need any more guilt. If there is a bent fork mutilated by the disposal, we take it. If we fry an egg and the yolk breaks, we know it's ours. We give the lean ham to our husbands, the front seat to our mothers, the last piece of pizza to our children.

It is a small wonder our offspring became the "me" generation. They were stigmatized by a martyred mother who cut her own hair but paid $60 an hour for her daughter to learn how to throw a baton and break every lamp in the house.

There is going to be a time that your kids say to you – "You don't love me!" When your kids are old enough to understand the logic that motivates a parent, you need to tell them this:

I love you enough to insist you buy a bike with your own money, even though we can afford it.

I love you enough to stand over you for two hours while you clean your bedroom, a job that would have taken me 15 minutes.

I love you enough to accept you for what you are, not what I want you to be.

But most of all, I love you enough to say no when you hate me for it.

You can't shield your kids from tough times. And, really, when tough times hit, kids can be pretty remarkable.

I was asked to write an inspirational book about children fighting cancer. I wondered if an optimistic book on cancer was possible.

I had always thought there are some subjects you just don't poke fun at. I was wrong. These kids had contests to see who could go the longest without upchucking after chemo. And one four-year-old confided in me, 'These people don't know what they're doing. They put blood in me one day and take it out the next.'

Right after the book came out – irony of ironies – I had my own cancer scare. The night before my surgery, I stood in front of a mirror and just stared at myself. Hey, two breasts aren't something I listed on my resume, for crying out loud. They're just a part of my anatomy that supports a name tag.

As I was leaving the hospital, a well-intentioned nurse handed me an envelope. *(Whispering.)* "Just slip this into your bra and you'll feel more balanced." As Bill drove me home, I opened the envelope. A small wad of cotton fell out. "My God! I've got dust balls under my bed bigger than this."

I did need a few more hours without interruptions, so I started interviewing household help. But guess what? No one wanted to be paid for what I had been doing for free.

(Sound: Phone ringing.)

(ERMA *moves to the bedroom and answers the phone.)*

Hello? Oh hi, Charmaine.

(To audience.)

This call from my neighbor changed my life.

(Into phone.) A lecture at the library? Sign me up. I'd go to a lecture on the history of the paper clip just to get out of the house. Betty Friedan? Never heard of her.

(ERMA *hangs up the phone. She takes the chair from the table, and drags it to the front of the stage.* **BETTY FRIEDAN**'s *voiceover runs as* **ERMA** *moves.)*

BETTY FRIEDAN. *(Voiceover.)* It is a strange stirring, a sense of dissatisfaction, a longing that women are suffering now. Each housewife struggles with it alone. As she makes the beds and shops for groceries, she is afraid to ask even of herself the silent question - 'Is this all'?

ERMA. *(To audience.)* Look at this library, it's full of women. Many of my neighbors are here.

(ERMA *sits and looks up expectantly at a speaker.)*

BETTY FRIEDAN. *(Voiceover.)* Telling bored, trapped, desperate, empty women that 'we're all in this together' is not a joke. Those housewife humorists who pretend it is are wrong. This is not funny! They revel in a comic world of children's pranks and eccentric washing machines and parents' night at the PTA. There is something about these writers that reminds me of Uncle Tom or Amos and Andy.

ERMA. Betty Friedan made me mad.

(**ERMA** *drags the chair back to the kitchen.*)

She shouted at us, "You are not using your God given abilities to their potential." She told us to erase forever the words, "just a housewife." I had a husband and three kids whom I loved. What was I supposed to do? Walk out? Join the circus? The next day, I bought *The Feminine Mystique* and read it cover to cover.

That book hit part of me I didn't even know was there.

Betty Friedan's words were ringing in my head. A week later, I found myself looking at an obituary in our local paper. My neighbor had died and the entire article was about her husband's and sons' accomplishments.

Have you noticed that if women make it into a news photograph, half the time they aren't identified?

No explanation – they just happen to be standing near some important man.

Betty Friedan had counted on an anger among women in her Midwestern audience that did not yet exist. We didn't realize it, but in those few hours, we had all been impregnated with the seeds of a movement of monumental proportions…one that would grow inside us and affect us all of our lives whether we embraced it or not.

When the fights over the Equal Rights Amendment started heating up, I was busy writing the column and driving the kids around.

The E.R.A. is only 16 words – "Equality of rights under the law shall not be denied or abridged on account of sex." It's astonishing that this concept isn't part of our nation's Constitution. I don't think any woman should go to her grave thinking E.R.A. stands for Earned Run Average.

I volunteered to go on the road with Liz Carpenter, who was the head of E.R.A. America. We were great, good friends, and we traveled together for two years, gathering wherever women gather – at beauty parlors and senior centers in states that hadn't ratified the amendment.

We spent time strategizing with Gloria Steinem and Bella Abzug. Did you know that Gloria, Bella and I all lost our fathers very early in life? We all saw what our mothers went through. My mom got paid less in the factory than the man working right next to her. Gloria said most women are just one man away from welfare.

I traveled on my own dime – it was my contribution to the cause – and I continued to keep up with my column three times a week.

My job was reasonably straightforward. It was to tell Americans that those 16 words simply meant "equality." When I was being flip, I told people "we've got to get sex out of the gutter and back into the Constitution where it belongs."

On the road, it often got interesting during our question and answer times.

(**ERMA** *moves downstage.*)

FEMALE QUESTIONER. *(Voiceover.)* Mrs. Bombeck, are you sure the E.R.A. won't wipe out any and all distinctions between men and women? What about unisex bathrooms?

ERMA. It won't. The only thing women have to fear from unisex bathrooms is that *we* will still be the ones cleaning them.

MALE QUESTIONER. *(Voiceover.)* Everyone knows your E.R.A. has a secret agenda and that's to destroy marriage and the American family. Why don't you mention that?

ERMA. Sorry but that's as phony as that comb-over. Next?!

MALE QUESTIONER WITH A SOUTHERN ACCENT. *(Voiceover.)* As our state's lieutenant governor, I'm pleased you are visiting our state and all, but Mrs. Bombeck, if you don't mind some unsolicited advice, why don't you just stay home and have babies?

ERMA. Well, sir, I did. And my babies now are old enough to vote against you.

(Sound: Applause.)

(ERMA walks back to the bedroom.)

One of my proudest moments was being appointed by President Carter to the National Advisory Committee for Women. It was a truly ground-breaking committee.

The President was asking us how to make things better for women in America.

Bella Abzug led the committee.

We gave our recommendations…and they shut us down.

When a draft of the report leaked out, Bella got fired. Most of us resigned in protest. It was called the Friday Afternoon Massacre.

And now, all these years later, many women still spend most of their paycheck on childcare.

While ordinary women were being clobbered by Washington, I was setting the record for the most widely distributed column in America.

Nine hundred newspapers! Who would have thought that writing about being a stay-at-home mom would have struck such a chord. The key to my writing is that I'm ordinary.

Everyone thinks of ordinary as some kind of skin disease. Face it. Most of us are not remarkable. We are not going to go to the moon. We're lucky to find the keys to our car in the morning.

I may never have won a Pulitzer, but I get top billing on kitchen refrigerators coast to coast.

(ERMA picks up the books on the shelf that is part of the bed's headboard.)

Aha! Economics: *I Lost Everything in the Post-Natal Depression.*

Ecology: *The Grass is Always Greener Over the Septic Tank.*

Sociology: *All I Know About Animal Behavior I Learned in the Loehmann's Dressing Room.*

Travel: *When You Look Like Your Passport Photo, It's Time to Go Home.*

Like most families, we fought the battles of the 70s at the dinner table. There were endless fights over hair length and short skirts. Bill was upset over a different kind of grass. All our kids considered employment a fad. Like mood rings. One kid spent so long in college, ivy grew up one leg.

It took a long time for our kids to find their own homes. Bill took to wearing a T-shirt that said: HOW CAN I SAY GOODBYE WHEN YOU WON'T LEAVE? As our silver wedding anniversary approached, I had visualized a dazzling gala with a large white tent and six-piece orchestra.

Several hundred guests would look on as Bill and I exchanged diamond tennis bracelets.

(**ERMA** *walks to the kitchen.*)

The reality was our kids threw a few hamburgers and hot dogs on the grill, scarfed them down and split, leaving Bill and me to clean up.

As much as I complained in print about staying home with the children, I loved it. If only I could have those kids back and re-live the year my youngest gave me a tattered picture of two hands folded in prayer. On it, he had crayoned this moving message: "Oh Come Holy Spit!"

Or that Mother's Day I got a shoebox that contained a baseball card and the gum was still with it.

The years of hands traced in plaster of Paris...the Christmas presents out of toothpicks and library paste... They're gone.

> (**ERMA** *walks to the bedroom and goes to the typewriter. She types and talks.*)

No more plastic tablecloths stained with spaghetti. No more bedspreads to protect the sofa from damp bottoms. No more gates to stumble over at the top of the basement steps.

You'll straighten up the boys' bedroom, neat and tidy: bumper stickers discarded, bedspreads tucked and smooth. Animals caged. You'll say out loud: "Now I want it to stay this way." And it will.

> (**ERMA** *ends typing.*)

No more anxious nights with a child under a vaporizer tent. No more sloppy oatmeal kisses. No knees to heal, no responsibility. Only a voice crying, "Why don't you grow up and act your age?" And then the silence echoing, "I did."

When I couldn't write about driver's ed and teenaged angst anymore, I thought maybe I should retire.

Instead, my husband and I decided to build a house. We argued over tiles, the water heater...even the closets.

Bill wanted a skylight over the shower. I could just visualize American Airlines flying low to give passengers a peek at my body.

And, we traveled. Vacations always sound so great on paper. The truth is, they are hard work. Bill is the kind of man who goes to the Grand Canyon and insists on stopping the car and getting out to take a picture, instead of rolling the car window down like everyone else.

When you get home, the important thing is to set fire to the contents of your suitcase. To me, a travel wardrobe has the same symbolism as maternity clothes. Get rid of them and you never have to go through the experience again.

I know it will only be a matter of time before Bill's beard is white fuzz, I grow a mustache and we're wearing matching glasses. No one will be able to tell us apart.

Not that I thought Bill and I would go through life like matched luggage. The only thing I had ever hoped for was that we would hate the same people together and deteriorate at the same pace.

I believe that a serious illness is a marriage's unspoken fear. But the chances of a couple staying healthy together and dying at the same time are Las Vegas odds.

I had been diagnosed with kidney disease in my twenties. Inherited from my dad. It wasn't an issue, really, for forty years. When it got worse, I worked darn hard not to make my treatment an issue.

In-home dialysis four times each day simply became part of my schedule. So the clock ticked a little faster for me.

The big surprise was that I was the first to stumble. It should have been the other way around. Insurance charts all but assured me that Bill's sell-by date would come first. But that didn't happen, Biff Blanchard.

> *(Sound: Breaking news intro "We interrupt this regularly scheduled program for this special report.")*

TV ANNOUNCER. *(Voiceover.)* This breaking news: The Equal Rights Amendment went down to defeat today, three states short of the thirty-eight needed to change the U.S. Constitution. Supporters of the amendment claim that anti-E.R.A. forces played on the same fears that had generated opposition to women's suffrage in 1919.

ERMA. Congress had given us seven years to persuade a majority of states to pass this amendment. Thirty-five states did…but we needed three more. We almost changed the Constitution.

I wish they could have put this on my tombstone: "She got Missouri for the E.R.A."

When Alice Paul wrote that original Amendment in 1923, she said each of us picks up a little stone and eventually you build a great mosaic.

> (**ERMA** *gestures toward her left, pointing outside the building.*)

At the United States Capitol, the Equal Rights Amendment is reintroduced every year. It's a ritual. Women lawmakers make sure it's the first bill in the hopper. And every year, nothing happens.

People wondered why, with all my success, I still kept up the column, the speech giving, the book writing? It wasn't for the money. Not a chance.

The truth is, I wrote all those years for me, and for the other mothers standing on their tiptoes in the back of the room, waving their hands to be recognized. I recognized them. It turned out that was my God-given talent, valuing what the rest of the world seemed to take for granted. I wrote for the moms, missing at the table, attending to all and maybe hoping for a shred of attention. Good old dependable, old faithful moms, ignored there in the back.

Even my mom was able to see that, although I suspected she used most of my books as doorstops.

If you asked her what was in my books, she was sorta vague. Kind of like when she tried to explain about menopause.

When I asked her what it meant, she said "Your baby basket dries up."

"Is that the clinical description?"

"That's what it amounts to."

Late in life, Mom and I became very close. It took a while for it to hit me that the roles of mother and child had reversed.

My mother is the most beautiful woman I have ever seen. The wrinkles in her face have been earned one at a time.

And her hands. They're small and veined. You can't help but be impressed when you see the ring finger has shrunk from years of wearing the same wedding ring.

Her naps are as frequent as mine used to be. She already has a sitter for New Year's Eve.

The transition comes slowly. Did it come the rainy afternoon when you were driving and you slammed on your brakes? And your arm sprang between her and the windshield and your eyes met with a knowing look?

Then, one day while my daughter was driving with me, she slammed on the brakes and her arm flew out, protecting me.

The switch had arrived.

So soon.

But that's what life is about, isn't it?

Who wants to live with regrets? Think of all those women on the Titanic who waved off the dessert cart.

My only regret in life is that I should have eaten more ice cream and less cottage cheese. And I shouldn't have worried what the dog thought when he saw me get out of the shower.

If I had my life to live over, I would have talked less and listened more.

I would have invited friends over to dinner even if the carpet was stained and the sofa faded.

Instead of wishing away that nine months of pregnancy, I would have cherished every moment and realized that the wonderment growing inside me was my only chance to assist God in a miracle.

When I stood before Him at the end of my life, I didn't want to have a single bit of energy or talent left. My plan was to wear out, not rust out.

I looked forward to saying, "I used everything you gave me."

But most of all, given another shot at life, I would seize every minute to make a difference...look at it and really see it...live it...and never give it back.

> (*The lights dim on the living room.* **ERMA** *moves to the area with the ethereal lighting and stands there in a pool of light. The light starts to fade but* **ERMA** *stops it with her next line.*)

Oh! When your mother asks, "Do you want a piece of advice?" it is a mere formality. It doesn't matter if you answer yes or no. You're going to get it anyway.

> (*The lights again start to fade, but* **ERMA** *has another thought, making the light return.*)

And another thing, marriage has no guarantees. If that's what you're looking for, go live with a car battery.

> (*The lights again start to fade, but* **ERMA** *has another thought, making the light return.*)

And always remember: Never go to your high school reunion pregnant...or they will think that's all you have done since graduation.

> (*The light holds too long, and* **ERMA**, *smiling, gives the OK sign to go dark.*)

> (*Blackout.*)

End of Play